First published in 1993
by HarperCollins Publishers Ltd
© Judith Kerr 1993
Reprinted 1996

Mog the Forgetful Cat was first published
by William Collins Sons & Co Ltd in 1970
© Judith Kerr 1970
Mog and the Baby was first published
by William Collins Sons & Co Ltd in 1980
© Judith Kerr 1980
Mog's Christmas was first published
by William Collins Sons & Co Ltd in 1976
© Judith Kerr 1976

ISBN 0 583 32775 3
The author asserts the moral right to
be identified as the author of this work

Printed and bound in China

The ADVENTURES of MOG

Judith Kerr

Collins

An Imprint of HarperCollins*Publishers*

CONTENTS

Mog the forgetful cat

Mog and the baby

Mog's Christmas

Mog the
forgetful cat

For our own Mog

Mr Thomas

Mrs Thomas

Nicky

Debbie

Once there was a cat called Mog and
she lived with a family called Thomas.
Mog was nice but not very clever.
She didn't understand a lot of things.
A lot of other things she forgot.
She was a very forgetful cat.

Sometimes she ate her supper.
Then she forgot that she'd eaten it.

Sometimes she thought of something
in the middle of washing her leg.
Then she forgot to wash the rest of it.

Once she forgot
that cats can't fly.

But most of all she forgot her cat flap.
The cat flap led from the kitchen
into the garden.
Mog could go out . . .

. . . and in
again.
It was
her
own
little
door.

The garden always made Mog very excited.
She smelled all the smells.
She chased the birds.
She climbed the trees.
She ran round and round
with a big fluffed-up tail.
And then she forgot the cat flap.
She forgot that she had a cat flap.
She wanted to go back into the house,
but she couldn't remember how.

In the end she sat outside the kitchen window
and meowed until someone let her in.

Afterwards you could always tell
where she had sat.
This made Mr Thomas very sad.
He said, "Bother that cat!"
But Debbie said, "She's nice!"

Once Mog had a very bad day.
Even the start of the day was bad.
Mog was still asleep.
Then Nicky picked her up.
He hugged her
and said, "Nice kitty!"
Mog said nothing.
But she was not happy.

Then it was breakfast time.
Mog forgot that cats have milk for breakfast.
She forgot that cats only have eggs as a treat.

She ate an egg for her breakfast.
Mrs Thomas said, "Bother that cat!"
Debbie said, "Nicky doesn't like eggs anyway."

Mog looked through her cat flap.
It was raining in the garden.
Mog thought, "Perhaps the sun is shining in the street."
When the milkman came she ran out.
The milkman shut the door.

The sun was not shining in the street after all.
It was raining.
A big dog came down the street.
Mog ran.
The dog ran too.

Mog ran right round the house.
And the dog ran after her.
She climbed over the fence.
She ran through the garden
and jumped up outside the kitchen window.
She meowed a big meow,
very sudden and very loud.

Mrs Thomas said, "Bother that cat!"
Debbie said, "It wasn't her fault."

Mog was very sleepy.
She found a nice warm, soft place
and went to sleep.
She had a lovely dream.
Mog dreamed that she had wings.

She could fly everywhere.
She could fly faster than the birds,
even quite big birds . . .
Suddenly she woke up.

Mrs Thomas said, "Bother that cat!"
Debbie said, "I think you look nicer without a hat."

Debbie gave Mog her supper
and Mog ate it all up.
Then Debbie and Nicky went to bed.

Mog had a rest too,
but Mr Thomas wanted to see the fight.
Mr Thomas said, "Bother that cat!"

Mog thought, "Nobody likes me."
Then she thought, "Debbie likes me."
Debbie's door was open.
Debbie's bed was warm.
Debbie's hair was soft, like kitten fur.
Mog forgot that Debbie was not a kitten.

Debbie had a dream.
It was a bad dream.
It was a dream about a tiger.

The tiger wanted
to eat Debbie.
It was licking her hair.

Debbie shouted. Mog jumped.
Mr and Mrs Thomas said,
"Bother, bother, BOTHER that cat!"
Debbie said nothing.
She was still crying because of the bad dream.

Mog ran out of the room
and right through the house
and out of her cat flap.
She was very sad.
The garden was dark.
The house was dark too.
Mog sat in the dark
and thought dark thoughts.
She thought, "Nobody likes me.
They've all gone to bed.
There's no one to let me in.
And they haven't even given me my supper."

Then she noticed something.
The house was not quite dark.
There was a little light moving about.
She looked through the window
and saw a man in the kitchen.
Mog thought, "Perhaps that man will let me in.
Perhaps he will give me my supper."

She meowed her biggest meow,
very sudden and very, very loud.
The man was surprised.
He dropped his bag.
It made a big noise
and everyone in the house woke up.

Mr Thomas ran down to the kitchen
and shouted, "A burglar!"
The burglar said, "Bother that cat!"
Mrs Thomas telephoned the police.
Debbie let Mog in
and Nicky hugged her.

A policeman came and
they told him what had happened.
The policeman looked at Mog.
He said, "What a remarkable cat.

I've seen watch-dogs,
but never a watch-cat.
She will get a medal."
Debbie said, "I think she'd rather have an egg."

Mog had a medal.
She also had an egg every day for breakfast.
Mr and Mrs Thomas told all their friends about her.
They said, "Mog is really remarkable."
And they never – (or almost never) –
said, "Bother that cat!"

THE END

Mog
and the
baby

For Ben Davis, who is very fond of cats

One day Mog was playing with Nicky.

Debbie was going to school.
Mr Thomas was going to work,
but Nicky had a cold.

Mog and Nicky played
Catch the String.

Then they played Bad Dogs.

Then they played Tickle Mog's Tummy,

and then they played ball.

Suddenly they heard a noise.
It was a crying noise
It was a very loud crying noise.

Mrs Thomas said, "Look who's here.
Mrs Clutterbuck has brought us her baby.
We're going to look after it while she goes shopping."

The baby looked at Mog
and stopped crying.
It said Psss instead.

"It's trying to say puss,"
said Mrs Thomas.

"Will my baby be all right with your cat?" said Mrs Clutterbuck.

"Oh yes," said Mrs Thomas. "Mog loves babies."

But Mog and Nicky had to stop playing ball
because the baby did not know how to play.

"I've got a very good idea,"
said Mrs Thomas. "Let's take
the baby for a ride in the pram."

The baby liked riding in the pram.
It said Psss.
"I've got a baby in a pram too," said Nicky.
Mog said nothing, but she was not happy.

When they came back it was lunch time.
But the baby did not want to eat its lunch.
It said Psss instead.

It said Psss and cried.
It cried so much that Mog did not
want to eat her lunch either.

She went away and
sat in her basket.

She sat in her basket
and tried to think of
other things, while
Mrs Thomas and Nicky
cleared the dishes.

The baby found a dish to clear, too.

"Look what it's done," said Nicky.

"Oh dear,"
said Mrs Thomas.
"Perhaps the baby
would like a rest."

But the baby did
not want a rest.
It said Psss Psss Psss.
It said Psss and cried.

"It wants Mog,"
said Mrs Thomas.

"Will Mog be all right
with the baby? said Nicky.

"Oh yes," said Mrs Thomas. "Mog loves babies."

Mog sat in her basket, and the baby stopped crying.
It was nice and quiet when the baby stopped crying.
It was so quiet that Mog fell asleep.

She had a dream.
It was a lovely dream.
It was a dream about babies.

SUDDENLY ... she woke up.

Mog thought,
this baby is everywhere.

She thought,
I'm getting out.

Mog ran across the road,

but the baby was coming after her,

and a bad dog was waiting
on the other side,

and there was a car coming.

"There's my baby!" shouted Mrs Clutterbuck.
"There's Mog!" shouted Debbie.
There's only one way to go,
thought Mog, and she jumped.
She jumped away from the dog.
She jumped away from the car.
She bumped into the baby.
The baby flew through the air
and came down on the pavement.
It said Psss.
Mr Thomas stopped the car just in time.

"My baby! Oh, my baby!" said Mrs Clutterbuck.
"It's a silly baby," said Nicky.
"It shouldn't have run into the road."
"Mog saved it," said Debbie.
"She is a very brave cat," said Nicky.
"She is the bravest cat in the world. She is a
baby-saving cat, and she should have a reward."

They all went to get Mog a reward.
It was a very big reward.
It was a reward from Mrs Clutterbuck.

"Mog saved my baby from being run over,"
said Mrs Clutterbuck.
"I told you," said Mrs Thomas, "Mog loves babies."

THE END

Mog's
Christmas

For my friend Mrs Cleghorn

One day Mog woke up
and nothing was right in her house.

Everybody was busy.
Debbie was busy.

Nicky was busy.

Mr and Mrs Thomas
were busy.

And there were too many
people in the house.
There was a jolly uncle

. . . and two aunts
on tippy-toe.

Mog thought, "I don't like it here."
She went and sat outside on the window-sill.
There was nothing to do and no one to play with
so after a while she went back to sleep.

Suddenly she woke up.
She saw something.
It was a tree.
It was a tree walking.

Mog thought, "Trees don't walk.
Trees should stay in one place.
Once trees start walking about
anything might happen."
She ran up the side of the house
in case the tree should come and get her.
"Come down," shouted the tree.
"Come down, Mog!"
"First it walks," thought Mog,
"and now it's shouting at me.
I do not like that tree at all."
And she ran right up to the roof.

The tree went on shouting for a while.
Then it went into the house.
Mog stayed on the roof.
Some white things fell out of the sky.
Some fell on the roof and some fell on Mog.
They were very cold.

At supper time
Mog was still on the roof.
"She must have her supper,"
said Debbie. "Mog always
has her supper."
Mrs. Thomas gave Mog her supper.
But still Mog did not come down.

In the morning Mog did not come down either.
She had found a nice tall place,
and she was asleep.
She was having a lovely dream.

Mog dreamed that she was sitting on a cloud.
Some white things were falling out of the sky.
Mog tried to catch them.
She was very happy.
But suddenly the cloud began to melt . . .

Inside the house everyone was sad
because Mog would not come down.
They were too sad to eat their breakfast.

Even the jolly uncle was sad,
and one of the aunts cried.

Suddenly there was a noise.
It was a noise in the chimney.
And then something came down it.
It came right down the chimney
and fell into the fireplace
with a thump.

"It's Father Christmas!"
cried one of the aunts.
"No, dear," said the other aunt,
"Father Christmas does not have a tail."
Debbie cried, "It's Mog!"

Then everything was lovely.
The whole house was lovely.
The tree had stopped walking about
and had made itself all pretty.
And Mog had three boiled eggs
and some turkey
and a present to unwrap.

"Happy Christmas, Mog," said Debbie.

THE END